baae

W9-COY-387

# How to Lose a Groom in 10 Days

NOV - - 2018

# How to Lose a Groom in 10 Days

**A Runaway Brides Novella**

Catherine Mann
and
Joanne Rock

How to Lose a Groom in 10 Days
Copyright © 2015 Catherine Mann and Joanne Rock
Tule Publishing First Printing, March 2018

The Tule Publishing Group, LLC

ALL RIGHTS RESERVED

No part of this book may be used or reproduced in any manner whatsoever without written permission except in the case of brief quotations embodied in critical articles and reviews.

This is a work of fiction. Names, characters, places, and incidents are products of the author's imagination or are used fictitiously. Any resemblance to actual events, locales, organizations, or persons, living or dead, is entirely coincidental.

ISBN: 978-1-948342-85-8

# Chapter One

BUYING A WEDDING dress off the clearance rack twenty-four hours before the Big Day had not been Melanie Webb's brightest idea ever.

A size too small, the fabric had cinched her breasts even before she began hyperventilating from the growing fear that she'd made a huge mistake with her impulsive courthouse elopement. An elopement she never thought the groom would really follow through on.

Now, as the Orange County, Florida judge pronounced Melanie a married woman, the tea-length bridal gown worked like a Chinese finger trap. With a ruffle at the hem. The more she tried to drag air into her lungs, the tighter the dress became. The ruffle teased her legs with hints of freedom, of breaking free. If she didn't get out of the tiny courthouse "Wedding Room" soon, she'd die of tulle-related asphyxiation.

Or the suffocating guilt of hurting a truly terrific guy. Whichever came first.

"Congratulations," the craggy-faced judge monotoned with a lack of enthusiasm that suggested he'd officiated too many marriage ceremonies to give a damn anymore. He shoved a signed license across the desk. "Don't forget your paperwork."

The Certificate of Marriage came without fanfare. He'd allocated them all of two point five seconds for a "you may kiss the bride" moment, which really was okay since a romantic swoop into her new husband's arms would have been awkward given the line of people waiting impatiently to tend to whatever court business they had – some looking decidedly sketchy considering this was supposed to be their wedding day.

Were they really married? Had she even said "I do"? She'd been shaking so hard she didn't remember. She barely recalled that two point five second peck on the lips. Surely a wedding deserved more. A memory to store of kissing her mouthwatering six-foot-three second baseman for the Atlanta Stars who stood beside her. She'd never shared a kiss with Grady Hollis that hadn't been vividly memorable.

He grinned down at her now, unaware of her sudden panic attack or her dress woes. He'd offered to go all out and buy the bridal attire when they'd decided to tie the knot three days ago, but three days ago she still believed they wouldn't really wind up here. She'd been certain he'd get on a plane with his team to start the regular season and they'd both move on.

But since she'd been the fun, party girl for the past ten weeks, she hadn't wanted to be the one to blink first in the game of elopement chicken. So she'd bought the dress on her own, after telling him she didn't want to start their marriage as a baseball groupie cliché, cashing in on Grady's high paying career even though she worked multiple jobs to make ends meet.

The jack-of-all-trades existence she'd led since high school had been her choice. This marriage, however? She would have never chosen to marry a guy who hadn't mapped out a future—a guy so content to live in the moment she had no earthly idea what happened next.

"Guess we're official." Grady's brown eyes held the same mix of devilry and challenge that had turned her inside out two and a half months ago when they'd first met. One of those attraction at first sight moments, the kind a girl fantasized about. But for her, it had seemed real, that night he'd charmed her and a room full of kids with some sleight of hand tricks at a family mixer that kicked off his team's spring training.

She'd pulled childcare duty through an event services company because of her CPR certification. And although seasonal work in a Florida ballpark was nothing new to Melanie, Queen of Temp Jobs to supplement working in her father's restaurant, caring for the ten-and-under demographic had been completely out of her league. She'd thought Grady was a nice dad who took pity on her when he'd organized an impromptu ball game with the rowdy Stars' offspring, but—amazingly—he'd been a major league player, single, and flirting wildly with her.

Ten weeks later, she could still hardly believe it. Or that she'd just married him.

"Official?" she squeaked, her voice a breathless rasp with panic and form-fitting shapewear squeezing the ever-loving life out of her.

"You make a better Mrs. Hollis than I could have ever hoped for." His blue eyes went darker. Serious.

Any other woman on the planet would have swooned at the declaration. She felt her throat close. Her skin itched like she might be getting hives. Had she really just married a man she'd known for the extent of one spring training season? Yesterday, she kept thinking he'd back out of it before they really said "I do." She'd counted on it even, not packing up all her old apartment, certain he wasn't really serious.

How many pro ballplayers had she seen come and go from Kissimmee, flirting with the local girls for a few weeks before heading back to their real lives?

"I—" She couldn't breathe. Or think. Or even begin to imagine how she could carve out a life at his side when major leaguers lived on the road for the better part of eight months each year.

Had she used this marriage and this great guy as a means to finally escape Kissimmee? Her troubled family that she hadn't even invited to the wedding? She clutched her little bouquet of peonies tighter. They'd cost more than her dress, but Grady had surprised her with the flowers. Insisted.

Guilt surged faster than Grady's fans after a win.

"You deserve much more," she rasp-whispered, an underwire support jabbing her left breast like an accusing finger. "I'm so sorry."

He frowned. His hands lifted to cup her shoulders.

"What are you talking about?"

Wasn't it obvious? One of baseball's hottest rising stars had just eloped with a glorified temp worker who was so deep in a panic attack she couldn't draw a full breath.

Her eyes stung as she thought about all the ways she was about to hurt him. But wasn't it better for him to find out now what a mess she was inside than later? The marriage could be annulled. Right?

Behind them, the judge cleared his throat.

"Your paperwork?" Craggy Face lifted the certificate off his desk and waved it meaningfully in their direction. "And tell the next couple they may step forward, please."

Melanie didn't bother answering. As soon as Grady turned to retrieve the papers, she sprinted out of the Wedding Room as fast as her pink high heels would take her.

EVERYTHING ELSE IN Grady Hollis's life had come easily enough.

Hits. RBIs. Walk off homeruns. He'd made every team he'd ever tried out for. Impressed scouts with his skills defensively as much as with his bat.

So maybe this moment was the universe's way of reminding him to stay humble. Because it sure as hell was humiliating to watch his bride speed away from him like a base runner trying to avoid the tag. He'd be damned if he would chase Melanie through the Orange County courthouse building past other newlyweds snapping pictures of their nuptials. Those other brides were gazing longingly up into their grooms' eyes. Melanie hit the massive stone steps with so much speed she broke the heel on her shoe. She'd just pulled them off and ran faster.

The sports media would have a field day with this if anyone found out, damn it. He'd been so careful lining up this time off with the team's press secretary, arranging it so he could drive to Atlanta instead of taking the plane back. Couldn't Melanie have waited to freak out about their wedding until they were safely back in his truck? Or home in his apartment they'd shared for the last month, where they'd planned to celebrate their honeymoon before for at least a few hours?

Then again, if they'd made it to a bed, she wouldn't have run in the first place. The chemistry they shared was too off the charts.

"Grady Hollis?" a woman shouted to him from the base of the stone staircase as he started down the steps.

His head swiveled automatically.

On the first floor, a woman raised her arm to point at

him.

"It's Grady Hollis, the Stars player!" she squealed.

Crap, crap, crap.

He thought about searching for a back staircase, but heads were already turning. Other people pointed. The guy in front of him on the stairs halted and spun around.

"Grady Hollis?" His southern accent drawled thick as he surveyed Grady's dark suit and tie. "Look here, boys." The older man yanked on the hands of a couple preschoolers who both wore Stars caps. "It's the ballplayer you saw with Grampy in spring training last week."

Grady searched the pedestrian traffic on the ground floor while a sea of workers heading for lunch break rolled out of the Orange County office buildings. Off to one side, he spotted a flash of white streaking toward the glass doors that led toward the parking lot.

"Can you sign my shirt, mister?" a tall, lanky kid with a scratchy voice asked from behind his left shoulder, already pulling off his tee.

"I saw you hit that humdinger at Stars Stadium against the Aces," someone else shouted from a few steps away—a heavyset guy with a briefcase under his arm and a coffee in one hand. "Do you remember that one? It went right over their centerfielder's head at the wall."

"You're really a baseball player, young man?" a grandmotherly type with steel-gray hair asked from his right, her weathered hand landing on his suit sleeve and preventing him from taking another step. "We root for the New York team in my house, but I'll bet my grandson would love to hear how I met a real baseball player."

The woman dug in a purse, presumably for a pen, while hats, papers and hands came at him from all sides, pressing him closer to the railing, pinning him onto the staircase with a gridlock of people. Damn it. Melanie wouldn't just leave him here, would she?

He grabbed a pen and a hat and started autographing things, making small talk on autopilot. He had no flipping clue what had happened back in the Wedding Room. Melanie had spent the night before at her parents' place even though they'd been living together for weeks. He hadn't thought twice about it, figuring all brides were superstitious about not seeing the groom on the day of the wedding until the ceremony. Totally normal, right?

Except maybe she had looked jittery during the ceremony. Fidgety. Breathing fast. But he'd figured all that was par for the course with brides. She knew he was crazy about her. What had gotten into her?

"Whatcha all dressed up for?" a teen with a pierced nose asked while she chomped on a piece of gum. "Traffic court? My mom said they don't care what you wear."

Grady kept signing and shuffled down a step as the dad with two little kids moved away. On a good day, Grady could sign autographs for a long time, grateful to work in his dream job and all too aware he was a lucky man. But right now, he needed to get to Melanie.

"Just watching a buddy tie the knot," he hedged, determined to keep his nuptials secret or he'd never get out of the building.

"Oh my God!" the girl squealed and so did ten other nearby women.

The noise level in the throng around him kicked up a few decibels. And a few octaves.

"Was it that nice Boone Sullivan?" The gray-haired granny next to him asked about the Stars third baseman, still clutching his arm while fans crowded them both. "He's supposed to marry a reality show actress."

"It wasn't anyone on the team," Grady rushed to explain. His teammates were going to string him up by his cleats for starting rumors. "But I'd better catch up to the wedding party now."

He signed the grandmother's coffee shop napkin that she'd found in her bottomless purse and gently disengaged himself. The crowd pressed closer, sensing they were losing him.

"Just one more!" a handful of people shouted in unison.

Instead, he dug his phone out of his pocket and held it up as he kept edging down the steps.

"Sorry. My friends are wondering where I disappeared to," he lied, knowing there were no messages waiting for him since the device hadn't vibrated in the last ten minutes. "I'd better get back to them."

"Only three days until the regular season starts, folks!" an old-timer called from the back of the group. "Better let this boy get on his way so he can pack his things and get to Atlanta."

Grady waved his thanks at the older man who balanced with the help of a cane.

"That's true, sir." He had a special place in his heart for the savvy fans who knew more about baseball than him. Some of the volunteers at the Orlando spring training facility had seen more baseball greats come and go than Grady would ever meet. "I've got a lot to do before the trip north."

Some of the people eased back, giving him enough room to make it to the bottom of the steps.

"Good luck, son," the older man called. "Travel safe."

The well wishes were echoed by a dozen other people before Grady broke free and arrived at the glass doors. He sprinted out to the parking lot, not giving anyone else time to recognize him. He scanned the area, remembering where he'd seen Melanie's economical four-cylinder Honda earlier. He'd parked one row behind her.

Only now, he spotted his truck easily enough. Her silver compact was nowhere in sight.

"Damn it." He cursed a whole lot more as he punched in her number, wishing he could have found a way to break free of the fans faster. Had she waited for him long?

"Hi, this is Melanie..." Her voice mail picked up after four rings.

Really?

She hadn't just ditched him after the wedding. Now she wasn't answering his calls?

He'd never been so confused. Opening the driver's side door of his truck he slid into the front seat and tried calling again. And again.

No answer.

What was it she'd said before she left? *You deserve so much more.*

What did that even mean? From the first moment he'd laid eyes on Melanie Webb, all he wanted was her. He came from a driven family of competitive athletes where winning was prized at all costs. Melanie's playful spirit and easygoing demeanor were like breathing fresh air.

Being with her made him feel—maybe for the first time ever—like he didn't have the weight of the world's expectations sitting on his chest every second of every day. With her, he could have fun. Not only did he love her something fierce, he wasn't sure he could face the regular season without her in his life.

After his fifth phone call went unanswered, he switched screens on his phone and started texting.

*I love you.* Without waiting for an answer, he kept typing and sent another message.

*Please talk to me.*

Outside his truck windshield, the commuter traffic had slowed. The parking lot was full but quiet. Still.

He waited. And waited.

It was worse than watching one of those slow pitchers work the late innings in a tie game. Time crawled by.

They'd just *married* for crying out loud. How could she—

His cell phone chimed. There was a message from "The Mrs.," a title Melanie had given herself when she'd messed around on his phone two days before. The same day she'd changed her ringtone to "Going to the Chapel." She'd had so much fun with the wedding, never once complaining about the quick ceremony or the lack of planning time the way most women would.

*This was a mistake.*

The words sucked the air out of his lungs. He squinted down at them like he'd read them wrong. But no… his wife had just told him she regretted marrying him less than an hour after the fact.

Obviously, she didn't know him as well as he thought she did. Because Grady Hollis didn't give up on anything. It made him a great ballplayer and sometimes, a truly stubborn ass. He hoped one day it would make him a great husband too.

For right now though, he remembered that while Melanie had been playing with his phone, he'd gotten to play with hers too. Would she remember the app he'd asked her if he could download?

The Family Finder was a GPS link to loved ones. She would always know where he was and vice versa. He'd wanted it on her phone so she'd always know he was safe in his hotel for the night and not hanging out at strip clubs when the team travelled.

But right now? The app served a bonus double duty and told Grady exactly where to find his missing wife.

# Chapter Two

ALONE IN THE back parking lot of a rest area off the Florida Turnpike, Melanie swiped a tear off her phone.

It had seemed cruel to keep ignoring Grady's calls, but she was in no position to talk coherently. After leaving the Orange County courthouse she'd jumped in the car and started driving. She'd chosen the Turnpike to put distance between her and what she'd just done. But she had no idea where she was going. She'd pulled over into a rest stop when Grady's texts had started coming in so she could read them and reply.

Now, she unbuckled her seatbelt so she could pull on a sweater over the clearance sale dress that had nearly sucked the life out of her back at the courthouse. The cinching bodice had eased a little once the hyperventilating stopped, but she'd also cheated and edged the zipper down a few inches to give herself some room.

Outside her car, a man walked with a small dog on a leash. Melanie double-checked that her doors were locked even though there were others at the rest stop. She might be having a breakdown, but she had her wits about her enough to keep an eye on her surroundings. Keep herself safe.

Or at least, she managed to protect her *physical* safety. She hadn't been smart enough to protect her heart from a certain charming athlete with a killer smile. Hadn't her mother told her she'd better be careful of the ballplayers? That had been back when she'd taken her first part time job at another spring training facility when she was just twenty years old. She hadn't had the time or the finances to go to college with her father's restaurant teetering on bankruptcy and her mom's drinking escalating. So Melanie had waitressed for her dad, helped keep an eye on her mom and picked away at an online degree that—God willing—she'd finally receive at the end of this summer.

Her father had been a promising college athlete once, so her mom understood the appeal. They were a baseball family, after all. Die-hard fans. But shoulder surgery had sidelined Melanie's father and he'd spent years circling through farm teams without ever making a big league roster again. He'd taken it hard, but he'd recovered. Melanie's mom, on the other hand? Still bitter.

Was it any wonder she hadn't told her parents about Grady? It would be a drama worthy of a Jerry Springer episode. Her cell phone dinged from a drink holder, the charger connected. She scooped it up.

*Our marriage was NOT a mistake.* A second message arrived on her phone with a cheerful chime. *We need 2 talk.*

Talk? She wasn't sure she could even string together coherent thoughts much less speak.

Hell, she wasn't even sure where she was. She'd just driven. She looked around the rest stop outside her windshield but didn't see any tips. Just the standard brick bathrooms. Vending machines. And picnic tables.

Her eyes went to the GPS that Grady had bought for her twenty-sixth birthday. She wasn't entirely sure what it was telling her about her location, but then she hadn't read the manual. What made him think she'd ever be able to handle life as a major league player's wife when she couldn't even navigate her way around her home state? She'd been too busy crying her eyes out to notice the signs along the highway.

She still couldn't believe he'd really wanted to marry her. He *had* married her, for crying out loud. Who did that?

As she felt around the console for her box of tissues, her eyes fell to the floral bouquet on the passenger seat. The whole car smelled like peonies. She dabbed her eyes and picked up her phone again.

*Don't worry about me*, she typed with shaking fingers. She needed to show Grady that he was wrong about her. About marriage. *Go to Atlanta and settle in your new place.*

He'd needed a moving service to transport his things to Atlanta ahead of them. She'd been able to fit half of her stuff in the trunk and back seat of her dinky car, a sad testament to how little she owned. How vastly their lifestyles differed.

She didn't just have cold feet. She was frozen all the way through.

Her phone chimed again.

*I'm not leaving town without you*, his next text informed her. *We chose that house together.*

Right. And since he'd been in Atlanta sending her pictures of houses as he drove around town with a realtor, he had missed the almost-panic attack she'd had then too. But back then, a whole month ago, she hadn't even been thinking about those homes as a place for *them* as a couple. Marriage hadn't even entered her head four weeks prior. She'd just been helping him choose a cool place to live because he was a hot guy and she'd been wild about him.

Knowing that he would move on without her in a kick-butt home in Atlanta while she stayed behind in Kissimmee had hurt at the time, but at least it had seemed… imminent.

To get married instead? Total ill-advised craziness. She'd figured it was just another fun adventure like when they danced in the rain on the ball field one night after the rest of the team went home. Or like the time she'd dared him to see how far he could launch a ball she pitched to him and he'd broken his neighbor's window. It had just been fun. Goofy. A spring training romance with an expiration date.

The phone was heavy in her hand as she typed.

*I chose the house for you*, she reminded him in her next text.

She'd used a lifetime of knowledge about travelling ballplayers and steered him toward a place equidistant from the stadium downtown and the private airfield used by the team.

The neighborhood was appropriately affluent to give him privacy but not so stuffy that he couldn't have a big backyard barbecue with some of the rowdier teammates. It had a guest house in case his parents wanted to visit him and three garages since she'd never known a major leaguer who was content with just one vehicle.

The next incoming message lit up. *Then we'll choose a different one together*, he replied. *For both of us.*

Melanie squeezed her phone so hard she accidentally shut off the screen. How could he be so freaking nice to her after she'd just ditched him at the courthouse? Clearly, he didn't get it. Didn't get her.

She'd done too good of a job hiding her deepest insecurities. Her true self. Even her family. Closing her eyes, she knew she had to stop this farce of a marriage before it went any further. For his sake as much as hers.

*I can't do this*, she texted and set aside her phone.

Enough was enough.

Reaching for the rear view mirror, she tilted it down to look at herself. Her mascara had smeared spectacularly. A tissue wasn't going to cut it. She dug in her glove box for a wet wipe and tried not to get the alcohol too close to her eyes.

*Owww.*

It stung anyway. Damage done, she swiped the cloth over the rest of her face, not wanting to see any remnants of the careful makeup job she'd done in her old, empty apartment that she'd kept even after she moved in with Grady last month. She'd known even then it was a temporary move. She'd told him she was spending the previous night at her parents' place, unwilling to admit that she'd kept the old apartment and spent the night before waiting for him to call and break it off. That's what spring training guys did. They broke it off when their real life called at the beginning of April.

She'd woken this morning disoriented from lack of sleep, still half expecting Grady to show up at the courthouse with a perfect "last date" planned—maybe take photos in the wedding finery and ride around town with cans tied to his bumper. She sure hadn't expected they'd really be married.

Now, she disassembled her wedding hairstyle, pulling out pins from the "Perfect Updo" she'd copied from a magazine. It hadn't come out the same since her dark hair only reached her chin, but it had been fun to try.

Too bad she was done playing dress-up. In all aspects of her life.

*Damn* her eyes stung.

*Knock, knock.*

The rap on her window scared a scream out of her. Wrenching her burning eyes open, she saw … Grady?

His poster perfect face stared back at her through the windshield.

Her heart still racing from the scare, she couldn't process what she saw. But it was him—her too-handsome-for-his-own-good superstar ballplayer in a tuxedo custom-tailored to his absurdly athletic body. His dark hair was freshly cut, a fact she hadn't noticed during their wedding ceremony. He must have gone to the barber yesterday. The cleft in his chin seemed deeper, his jaw set. His pickup truck was parked in front of her Honda, blocking her exit from the rest stop.

*Oh God.*

It was one thing to ignore his calls and texts. Grady Hollis was not the kind of man she could ignore in person. Just looking at him—even through eyes that pricked with tears of pain—made her chest hurt with wanting him.

Swallowing hard, she blinked fast to try and clear her vision as she rolled down the window. A cool afternoon breeze blew in along with the scent of a nearby mimosa tree.

"How did you find me?" Her voice cracked, her throat a little hoarse from the crying she'd done on the turnpike.

He flipped the screen of his phone toward her so she could see it. A red dot blinked on a map.

"I put the Family Finder app on your phone that night when you took mine to change my ringtone, remember? I figured the next time you got lost or needed directions, I'd be able to help you out." He shoved the phone in his pocket.

"Instead it led you right to me." Not everyone was as directionally challenged as her. She'd lived in and around Kissimmee and Orlando all her life and she still got lost more than Grady.

"Funny thing that. I wanted to be with my wife on our

wedding day." He reached through the window to brush a finger along her cheek. Tilt her chin up. "What happened to your eyes?"

His touch made her heart skip a beat. Same as always.

But dang inconvenient when she needed to prove to him that marriage was a mistake.

"I used an alcohol wipe too close to my eyes." The sting had eased but she could only imagine what a bloodshot mess she had going on. She took hold of his hand to move it carefully aside, resisting the urge to curl her fingers around his and link them. "Grady, I ran from the wedding for a reason—"

"Can we talk about this in the car?" He looked over his shoulder toward a couple stumbling through the woods as they tried to hold on to the leashes of matching St. Bernards. "I'd rather not advertise our discussion."

Right. Him being famous and all that. She'd been with him more than once when a seemingly lone fan suddenly multiplied into fifty people waving ball caps, cocktail napkins and occasional exposed body parts in his face.

"I guess," she said begrudgingly, "but it's important you understand that I only want to—"

She gave up her speech since he'd already jogged around to the passenger side. She reached over to pull up the lock hoping it wasn't a mistake to let him in. But she needed to explain to him why they were all wrong for each other. Why they shouldn't have gotten married in the first place. And perhaps that was something a woman shouldn't do via text.

"Thanks." Angling his broad shoulders inside, he lowered his unfairly scrumptious body into the seat beside her, shoving aside the peonies so they didn't get crushed. He peered over the head rest at her clothes, blankets and personal stuff crammed in the backseat. "Not much room in here, is there?"

His gaze darted briefly toward his roomy, late model pickup truck sitting just outside.

She bristled. "We can't all have million dollar contracts and the new vehicles that come with them."

Her Honda had gotten her through a lot of lean years. A lot of late night runs to bars around town to retrieve her mom.

"But you can." He scooped up her hand in his and lifted it to his lips. "I want to share everything I have with you." He frowned down at her bare ring finger where he'd placed a beautiful diamond earlier that morning.

Clearing her throat, she tugged her hand back.

"No. You don't." She grabbed the wide collar of the gray cardigan she'd slid on over the wedding dress and hugged the cotton closer, determined to make him understand. "This speedy marriage was a mistake, Grady, and I'm going to prove it."

REALLY?

Grady stared across the console of the smallest car known to mankind and wondered what had gotten into Melanie. He knew they were right for each other. Knew it with a bone-deep certainty. Maybe his baseball career had fast-forwarded his dating life because he'd been with enough women to know beyond any doubt—quirky, free-spirited Melanie Webb was it for him.

No more trials needed. She was The One.

But it seemed she was ready to shake him off. Like a hitting slump. Or a losing series on the road.

Too bad he had no intention of going anywhere.

"I think you've got an indefensible position there," he observed, wishing they were exploring positions of another kind altogether. Didn't have to be Kama Sutra or anything crazy. Just having her in his arms was enough.

His gaze dropped to where she clutched her sweater around her generous curves. He'd missed her in his bed last night. Had consoled himself that he'd be celebrating their marriage with her by this time today. He could tell the moment when she started feeling the vibe—maybe he'd stared a little too long. She straightened in her seat and loosened the hold on the sweater.

"It's very defensible." She licked her lips, her dark brown eyes roving over his chest for just a moment before she twisted in her seat to face front. "We're way too different. You're going to be living on the road, seeing the country, being courted by the press, fans, potential sponsors who want you to hawk their wares—."

"I've already lived that," he reminded her. "This isn't my first year in the majors."

"But you've hardly reached the peak of your career. You're just getting started. And the way you're going, you're only going to be more and more sought after. As for me?" She shook her head and slumped in her seat. "I'm only just getting an online degree. I have no means to support myself and—before you interrupt with generous offers of help—I wouldn't be happy being a kept woman. I need something of my own."

"So we're on different trajectories. You'll be ready to conquer the world when I'm ready to leave baseball. It will be my turn to help you while you live your dream."

"You don't get it." She frowned, her distractingly kissable mouth forming a plump pout. "You don't even know my dreams. How can you say if you'll help me achieve them?"

He needed to tread very carefully, but it was taking all his brainpower to focus on the words when what he really wanted to do was take her home and torch away all this confusion with the searing heat that blazed every time they touched.

"Do you know your dreams, Mel?" He loved this woman like crazy. Respected the hell out of her too. She carried the weight of her whole family on her shoulders from running her dad's restaurant more often than the man in charge, to cleaning up the daily dramas of her mother's drinking problem.

Of course, he only knew that in a peripheral sense from watching her in action. He'd never been invited to meet the Webbs, and maybe that in itself should have told him something. But that didn't mean he intended to let her walk away. He would reassure her and fix whatever the hell had gone wrong in the past twenty-four hours to spook her this badly.

"I know my dreams are very different from yours, Grady." She stared out the windshield at a gray-haired couple taking their time exiting a sedan, moving carefully on stiff knees as they headed toward the walking path close to Melanie's car. They leaned into one another, arms locked as if they held each other up.

"How do you know that?" Frustration simmered. He wanted to be that old guy whose girl still stood by him even when his batting average no longer claimed space on the sports page. "Because I think our dreams are damn similar. We both want kids. We want dogs. We want a swing set and barbecues in the backyard with the neighbors."

He wanted the kind of life the kids around him had growing up but without all the pressure to perform the way he'd had from his sports-minded father. Melanie could give him that balance. Hell, she'd taught him it existed in the first place.

"You can't have a swing set when you're on the road for

two thirds of the year." She rubbed an idle touch over the place where her wedding ring had briefly rested. "It was fine when we both lived here, but your life here during spring training is just a blip on the player radar. Everything will change when we get to Atlanta and you're gone for two thirds of the year. I don't want to be a part time wife."

"So we'll make adjustments." He was trying his best here, but none of this made sense to him.

She bit her lip.

"What?" he pressed. "I don't get it. Why didn't you bring any of this up three days ago? You didn't say anything about being a part time wife. You said yes, and made me the happiest damn man imaginable."

Still, she said nothing. He'd never seen her quiet for this long and it worried him.

"Talk to me, Mel—"

"I didn't think you were serious about this." Her softly spoken words chilled him.

"About what? I forked over a ring that cost as much as my car."

She shook her head. "I didn't think you were really serious about getting married. I thought—I don't know. It just seemed so out of the blue."

"I just spoke legally binding vows." He reeled. Had she thought marriage was a joke to him? "How much more serious could I be?"

"We didn't talk about the future or how it would work.

You've never met my family—."

Anger simmered.

"You didn't want me to meet your family." His shoulders tensed. Damn it, he knew she'd been too good to be true. "There's a difference. I thought we didn't talk about the future because you're the kind of person who lives in the moment. Didn't you tell me that's what you liked?"

"Yes." She pressed the heels of her hands against her eyes, as if she could shut out the day. Him. "But there's more to me than the girl who lives in the moment. Just because that's what I like to do doesn't mean I—. My life is more complicated than you know."

"So show me." He spread his arms as wide as her tiny car would allow. "It's go-time now. We're married, Melanie, and I'm not taking back that ring."

"What does that mean?" She eyed him warily.

"It means I want to understand this complicated life of yours. If we're so different you really think we're not meant to be together, let me see this mysterious other side of you."

"Now? Here?"

He shrugged. "Wherever. You decide."

"You have to be in Atlanta in three days," she reminded him. "You have a schedule to keep."

"Right. But I'm going to show you how serious I am about this right now. I'm not going anywhere until you start being honest with me."

HE WANTED HONESTY?

Melanie stared at the unmoving mass of muscle in the passenger seat and recognized the expression on his face. It was the same one he wore when he got down in the count to a good pitcher and he really dug in at home plate. That set to his jaw said he wasn't going anywhere.

"Fine." If he wouldn't listen to her, then she'd have to show him. "You want to know what my life is really like? You can come with me on my next big adventure." She turned the key in her ignition to start the car. "We'll see how long it takes you to go running back to your five star hotels and team travel secretary."

"Good. I welcome the challenge. If I stop off at the truck to grab a change of clothes, you won't peel out of the parking lot without me, will you?" His eyes roamed over her face as if searching for a trick.

"You blocked me in."

"Right. But after what happened at the courthouse, I've found you're quite the getaway artist."

She hated that she put that distrust there, but it was just another sign that she was all wrong for him. That he deserved better. She had no idea how to make a long term relationship work with a guy who would be gone most of the time.

"I'll wait for you." She didn't need to trick him. Once

she showed him all facets of herself, and not just the cleaned-up fun version she'd shared with him, he'd understand all too well why they weren't meant to be.

He'd never seen her childhood home or met her parents. Didn't know why she was the self-declared queen of temp jobs in Orange County, Florida. No employers in Kissimmee kept her on the payroll long since she was liable to run off at a moment's notice to pick up her mother after a bender or referee an argument down at the grocery store when her parents were causing a public stir.

Her life wasn't particularly fun—except when she was with Grady. And that was only because she'd carefully kept her family out of it.

She watched him jog back to his vehicle for a leather overnight bag. He thumbed the "lock" button on his truck before climbing back into her car and she pulled out of the rest area parking lot. She'd change out of her dress at the next fuel station since she was already low on gas.

"So, what makes you think you can send me running?" he asked, his broad shoulder brushing hers as he maneuvered around to get more comfortable in the seat.

"That's part of what you're going to learn over the next three days … or sooner, depending on how fast you cry uncle."

"Where are we going?" Dropping his keys in the center console of the Honda, he loosened his tie and unbuttoned the top fastening on his dress shirt.

Exposing more of the tanned column of his throat. The depression at the base of his neck that she liked to kiss. Lick.

She forced her eyes back on the road with an effort and took a deep breath to slow her rapid heart rate. Focus on the task at hand.

"We're going camping."

# Chapter Three

"I THINK WE goofed and put the right tent poles on the left side of the tent." Melanie double-checked the directions against the lopsided blue and gray canvas structure Grady had been working on for the last twenty minutes.

To his credit, he'd been endlessly patient with her decision to check into the state park on Lake Kissimmee, a place she used to go with her parents back in happier times. Grady hadn't minded leaving his truck behind or his worldly possessions. Hadn't winced when she'd mentioned hiking farther from the lake to have a more primitive camping experience, or even when she'd dug out her old backpack and the cheap tent she'd bought her first summer out of high school.

But she sensed his patience was wearing thin when she'd struggled to interpret the faded directions on the time-worn brochure that had been packed away with the tent. His shoulders had a definite stiffness, a fact she could see all too clearly as he tugged off his damp t-shirt. They'd changed out of their wedding finery at a gas station close to the Lake Kissimmee campground, but after hiking for an hour to their more remote location, even shorts and tees felt sticky on the hot afternoon.

No surprise that Melanie's skin heated even more as Grady peeled off that shirt.

"Maybe it would help if we looked up the instructions online instead of reading through an old marshmallow smudge." He picked up his phone and started inputting commands with flying thumbs. "There's no rule against utilizing digital help for problem solving in this wager of yours, is there?"

"There is no wager." She set aside the brochure and tried not to stare at the ridged muscles of his stomach or the dusting of light brown hair visible just above low-slung shorts. "I'm just trying to show you the other side of me. How would you feel if I wanted to go camping instead of staying in the team hotel while you were on the road?"

For that matter, what if she got a call from home and her mother needed bail money after a night in the drunk tank for some local dust-up when Mom turned ornery? How understanding would Grady be when she ran back home to put Band-Aids on the hemorrhaging wounds of the Webb clan?

"I would work harder to remind you why you'd rather sleep in my bed every night." He glanced up at her over his phone, the look he sent curling her toes.

Rendering her speechless.

Because he had the power to do just that. She knew it.

And he knew it. So she wouldn't go arguing that particular point and give him an opportunity to prove her wrong.

Pivoting away from him, she walked around the spot they'd chosen to camp, needing to walk off the tingling in her thighs and between her legs. She felt his eyes follow her, making the ache worse.

"Melanie," he called in that sexy smooth voice of his, "If you really wanted to camp while I was on the road, I'd lobby the team to let me spend that time with you."

"The Stars would never go for that." She knew how strict the major league clubs were about player curfews and team bonding.

"They're more lenient with family guys." Setting down his phone, he returned his attention to the tent poles, tugging two of them from their canvas sleeves to re-thread them in new places. "They know a player can't be happy if his family's not happy."

"Right. So they throw a little more money your way and hope the wifey will be content with a new car." She'd seen with her own eyes how tough life on the road could be for player wives—had been out socially with some of the younger ones in past years when she'd worked spring training events with the families. "That doesn't satisfy any woman who genuinely loves her husband and not his paycheck."

Although it would have made Melanie's mother happy. She'd stalked the spring training fields around town twenty-some years ago in hope of hooking up with a player and moving out of the Florida backwater town where she'd been born. Maybe that was part of what bothered Melanie about being with Grady. Her mother would make ugly assumptions about her and—worse—she'd crow to all of her barfly friends that her daughter struck it big by snagging a big-leaguer.

Her thoughts were so dark, she hadn't noticed that Grady had stalked closer. She felt his presence a second before he put his hands on her shoulders and gently turned her to face him.

"In that case, thank you for loving me more than my paycheck." His hands lingered on the bare skin just below her t-shirt sleeves.

Strong, warm hands. The touch scrambled her thoughts.

"What I mean is—" She licked dry lips, trying to recall what she'd meant.

"I know what you mean." His thumbs moved in the smallest of circles on her arms.

Her breasts beaded under her shirt, her whole body responding to his nearness. His voice.

"Maybe we shouldn't touch each other until we have this situation worked out," she suggested, her voice cracking while her whole body protested the idea.

"It feels good though, doesn't it?" He got his fingers involved in the light massage, the touch smoothing along the place where her bra straps rested, as if he was testing out her clothes to see how much he'd need to remove to get her naked.

Or was that wishful thinking on her part?

"It kind of clouds my thinking," she admitted, wondering if he'd hypnotized her with sex at some point. She definitely felt the potent power of suggestion right now.

"Mine too, but I like that feeling, Mel." He let his hands fall to his sides and took a step back. "Just make sure you let me know when we can start touching again."

She blinked, confused at the loss of his touch since her hormones were running wild. Clearing her throat, she tried to shake off the longing that weighed down her limbs. She needed to pull herself together. Stop acting like a love-starved teenager and remember what she was here to do—prove to Grady Hollis that the wedding was a mistake. Something she'd never do if she kept swooning every time he touched her, for crying out loud.

Marching over to her backpack to retrieve a nice, cold drink in an effort to cool herself off, Melanie noticed the whole thing was moving.

What the hell?

Her overstuffed backpack wriggled backward as if trying to get away from her.

"Grady?" she called, stopping in her tracks. What if there was a giant python under the pack? Or a baby alligator? Gators were known to hang out around central Florida watering holes.

Keeping a wary eye on the green canvas bag, she backed

up a step and ran smack into Grady.

"What is it?" He reached toward the bag before she could warn him.

He slid the sack toward them but the bag resisted, a little yellow furry tail wagging free from the side pocket. A canine tail, for sure. Laughing, Grady tugged the bag harder and revealed…

A fluffy Golden Retriever pup. The puppy rolled free from the bag, flipping over twice before popping up onto all fours again. Fearless in the face of discovery, the matted, dirty bundle barked twice, tail wagging so fast the furry butt moved in time.

"Oh, look!" Melanie was already reaching for the animal when Grady stopped her.

"Wait up." He pulled a hand towel out of the bag and passed the length of terrycloth to her. "Use this to hold it."

"He's not that dirty," she insisted, wanting to snuggle it in spite of herself. "How cute is he?"

"What if it's rabid?" Grady used the towel to carefully lift the wriggling pup and get a better look at it as he held the dog at an awkward arm's length. "Better not let those little teeth get close. And it looks like a 'her' to me."

"Rabid?" Chuckling, she plucked the puppy from his arms and promptly got a lick on the chin. "She's acting mighty friendly if you ask me." Melanie lifted the pup's gum and checked the tiny teeth. "She can't be but two to three months old. Most places a puppy can't get rabies vaccinations until they're at least twelve weeks old. I learned that on one of my temp jobs once answering phones at a vet clinic, but you can look it up on your awesome phone if you want." She couldn't resist the last jab.

"Ha, funny." He cocked an eyebrow at her, already typing away on his cell anyhow.

"And while you're at it, look up the nearest vet clinic so we can get flea prevention," she clicked through the details, for once in her comfort zone and feeling confident about something around this man, "a good dewormer, puppy vaccinations and check for a microchip."

"Dewormer?" He glanced at the pup in horror.

Finally, she'd rattled him. Who would have thought it would be over canine parasites? She stifled a slightly hysterical laugh. "Haven't you ever had a dog?"

"No, I can't say that I have," he said softly without looking up from the cell. "My parents said we spent too much time on the road with my sports and it wouldn't be fair to the dog. And now's no different so I don't have a pet."

"Sure it's different these days," she pressed, not even sure why she was bothering. It wasn't like they would be traveling with a pet together as husband and wife. "There are pet friendly hotels everywhere. Check the website bringdfido.com." She cast him a sideways look. "But then that's probably not okay since the team may not be staying there. Like with camping."

He lowered his phone. "You're leaving me because my

job isn't conducive to camping or having a dog?"

Shaking her head, she sagged back against a tree wearily. "Those are symptoms of a bigger issue. We live differing lifestyles. Our values differ."

That last part clearly pissed him off. She could see by the narrowing of his eyes. Would he stalk away and call for a limo to pick him up? She would have made her point and ... tears stung. She cradled the wrapped up puppy closer as their tent wobbled in the wind.

Grady's set jaw relaxed. "Do you want to stand here and argue or do you want to go to the vet?" He held up a phone again. "I have an address and GPS directions."

Of course he had directions. Without him, she would have been stuck asking the guy behind the campsite counter to draw a map on the back of a fast food bag. "Let's get this puppy checked over." She reached into the pocket of her sweater, fished out the keys and pitched them to him. "You drive. I'll hold Polly."

He shrugged, surrendering as he snagged the keys out of midair. "Polly, you're a lucky puppy to have met Melanie."

THAT NIGHT, DRIVING through a rain shower on their way to the campground after the visit to the veterinary clinic, Grady watched Melanie cradle the puppy with a tenderness that got to him. He'd seen that side of her once before—that first night when they'd met at the Stars' family event and she'd been in charge of the childcare room for the team members who needed an extra eye on their kids. Now, as she cooed and comforted Polly, Grady remembered yet another reason he wanted her in his life.

She'd be ten times the parent he ever would. His own parents had fought so hard about how to raise him that they never had enough time to just "be." His father always lobbied for more sports, more tournaments, more training. His mother wanted family time. Grady about came apart at the seams trying to make them both happy. But Melanie would never be like that.

Still, maybe it wasn't enough that he had faith in her parenting. They'd never talked about having kids—he just assumed. And if he were already reading her all wrong now, how would it be five years from now? It killed him to think he'd run headlong into a marriage that could end up as unhappy as his parents'. They had waited until his younger brother turned eighteen and filed for divorce the next day.

"Is she warming up?" he asked, the silence broken only by Melanie's soft words to the shivering dog on her lap and the rhythmic scrape of the Honda's worn wiper blades as the rain picked up force.

"I think so." She readjusted the towel she'd resurrected from a bag in her backseat as they drove toward the campground. "Her fur is dry now."

The pup had a quick bath to rinse off the dirt for the

vet's assessment. It turned out Polly had a microchip that led to a local shelter. There were records that the animal had current vaccinations, but the owners, sadly, weren't interested in retrieving their puppy. They said she was more work than they'd anticipated. They were tired of chasing her when she dug out of the backyard. Grady had bought some basic puppy supplies from the vet clinic's store, including food, a bowl and a cardboard carrier in the backseat, and packed up the little fur ball to bring with them.

His hands clenched around the steering wheel as he thought of that puppy out alone, how easily he could have been stolen or hit by a car. "They shouldn't have left her in the backyard all the time. She probably got bored out there with nothing to do, no human contact."

"You have the instincts of a good pet owner after all." Melanie leaned back in her seat, her gaze shifting to the dark, wet road ahead.

"You don't have to sound surprised." He downshifted as they approached a low spot on the road where the rainwater had pooled.

"I was paying you a compliment."

"Forgive me if I'm not sure what to read in your words today." He swerved to the far side of the road to try and stay out of the deepest part of the puddle. He wished he could navigate the potential pitfalls in this conversation half as easily. "Why did you name her Polly?"

"That was my first dog. She and I spent a lot of time together curled up in my room while my parents argued. She kept me company. She was my best friend and the best dog ever."

"What kind of dog was she?"

"Some kind of lab mix. I didn't think of her as a kind of dog though, just *my* dog."

"Your folks argued a lot?"

"Mom's an alcoholic. Dad enables. He tries to avoid arguments, but she could provoke a saint on the nights she moves from red wine to bourbon." She shook her head as if to stop herself from saying anymore. "Short answer – yes."

"I don't know what makes you think I'm only interested in the short answers, Mel. If we want any hope of sorting through what's going on between us, we're going to need to both… try."

The rain pounded the hood with new vengeance and he wished they'd taken his truck which could have sailed right through all the standing water on the old country route. But Melanie's car was low to the ground and the sudden wealth of puddles-turned-ponds threatened to swallow it.

"Wait." She gripped his sleeve before he could go around the next major body of water. "The car stalled on me last week when I got water in the distributor cap."

"Where was I?" Frowning, he stepped on the brake. He didn't remember and would have used it as an excuse to press his case to give her a new vehicle.

"Fundraiser for the children's hospital." She peered out

the back window, probably to make sure no one was behind them since he'd stopped in the middle of the road.

But it was a quiet area outside the state park. Or maybe everyone else just had enough sense not to drive in a downpour. He wondered if she knew she still had her hand on him. He liked that she touched him when she wasn't thinking about it—that her hands went to him if only in a subconscious way.

"It's your call." He put the power in her hands, knowing that she liked weighing in on things and he was trying to be the kind of guy she wanted. Needed. "Should I try going through or do we wait out the storm?"

Her eyes met his in the dim car interior, the tiny compact putting them so close their breath mingled just sitting next to each other. Awareness spiked along with his temperature. She must have felt it too because her hand fell away from his arm, her eyes going wide for an instant before she looked anywhere but at him.

"Might as well try to get through it. We're almost to the campground."

Where they'd have to hike a trail to get back to their tent. It hardly seemed fair to Polly, let alone to the two of them, but he'd be damned if he'd state the obvious.

Gritting his teeth, he nailed the accelerator. Water splashed high on the doors and he gunned it harder to get through the puddle fast. Just as his foot pressed more, however, the ignition sputtered. And died.

Leaving them stranded in a miniature lake.

He turned to check Melanie's reaction. She chewed her lower lip and stared out the window. He'd done his damnedest to do things her way. Now? They were going with his plan. It was his wedding night, after all.

Tugging his phone out of his pocket, he switched on the screen.

"What was that website you mentioned again? Bring-Fido.com, right?"

# Chapter Four

MELANIE CINCHED THE hotel robe tighter on her waist, the thick cotton chasing away any remaining chill from her dash through the rain from the car. Grady had braved the downpour to dry out the distributor cap and—miraculously—was able to restart the Honda. He'd insisted on a hotel though, and she'd agreed as much for Polly's sake as for her own. Their campsite would be washed out even though the rain had slowed in the last hour.

Now, checked into the luxury accommodations that gladly gave Polly her own bed, Melanie couldn't stop thinking about the fact that this was her wedding night. A strange wedding night, of course. And one that they wouldn't celebrate in the er—usual way—since she'd declared the whole thing a mistake. But as she stepped out of the bedroom and into the living area to see Grady balancing a room service menu on one knee, she couldn't help but fixate on how things could have been so much different right now if only she'd been willing to accept a part time husband. A man who would be out of her life for two thirds of each year.

A man who'd genuinely wanted to marry her.

Her heart squeezed at the thought.

"So you won. We're in a luxurious hotel." She snapped at him to keep herself from thinking about how at home he looked here in his snug-fitting cotton tee and a pair of running shorts.

The man had the best thighs on the planet. Best butt, too. That's where the power came from in his lethal swing, she knew. Those amazing glutes. She didn't even want to think about what those same good glutes had done for her sex life.

"A luxurious hotel that accepts dogs," he clarified, setting aside the menu while his eyes roamed over her. "I think I should get kudos for that. Especially given I'm spending my wedding night in a suite with two beds and a dog."

He'd gotten them a two-bedroom suite and she'd been grateful he hadn't pushed the issue at check-in. But obviously, the choice didn't make him happy.

"Sharing a bed would only make things more complicated when we get an annulment," she pointed out, her gaze falling to Polly where she gnawed on one of Grady's discarded running shoes.

She bent to retrieve the sneaker before the puppy put a hole in it.

"I'm definitely not talking about annulments on my wedding night." Grady glared at her. "What do you want from room service?"

"I don't care." She tossed the shoe in his bedroom and then shut the door to keep the pup out. It wouldn't be fair to teach Polly she could chew on whatever she liked—even though Grady's seemingly endless cash flow could replace just about anything. Even, probably, a wife. "Order whatever you want."

"Okay then, I'm ordering all your favorites." He reached for the TV remote, muscles on mouthwatering display as he stretched.

"You know my favorites?" She couldn't remember ever telling him something like that.

He set the remote on the arm of his chair and used it to scroll to a room service menu on the television screen.

"I know more about you than you give me credit for." He kept his voice even but something about that carefully controlled tone told her she'd touched a nerve.

He jabbed buttons harder as he input their room number.

"We've spent so little time together—"

"So you say. But I think ten weeks is plenty of time to get to know someone if you're paying attention the way I have been. Contrary to what you might think, I've been taking this relationship damn seriously." He clicked to the appetizers and checked off the fruit platter, hot spinach and cheese dip with an extra baguette, and a bowl of wonton soup—definitely the same three items she would have narrowed into her top choices. Except for the bonus baguette, which she would have craved but not ordered.

"Wow." Absently, she bent to scratch Polly's ears while the pup wrestled with a stuffed animal Grady had picked up in the hotel gift shop. "How did you know?"

Without answering, he jumped to the dinner screen and requested a small pizza—cheese only. The second meal included enough meat for a linebacker, and she knew that was meant for him. He consumed protein like breathing air.

At the end of the order, in the "additional comments or requests" section he used the keypad to highlight letters for "marshmallows and sticks."

She had to laugh. "They'll never stock sticks in the kitchen."

"It's a good hotel. They'll think of something." Tossing aside the remote, he met her gaze. Warm brown eyes teased over her body with ill-disguised heat. "You deserve a picnic since you lost your night of camping."

Touched that he would think of something so sweet, her eyes burned. Damn it, was it any wonder he'd persuaded her to marry him even though they didn't know each other? Even though she'd carefully hidden her mess of a past from him?

She'd wanted to buy into the fairy tale. To make the dream of them last for as long as possible, which was how she'd ended up breaking out in hives in a wedding dress that morning.

"Well. Thank you." She cleared her throat, determined

not to send him mixed signals. "I. Um. How did you know I liked all of those things you ordered for dinner?"

"Easy." He sat forward in his seat and tugged the stuffed gator from Polly's mouth. Shaking off a little puppy drool, he tossed the green stuffed toy a few feet away and they watched her chase the prize and tumble over it. "You debate out loud what you want to eat when you're looking at a menu," he informed her. "So I know the kinds of things you choose, plus the runners-up."

She couldn't recall meeting anyone who'd observed her so closely. Her parents had always been too consumed by their own drama to take an interest in her life. How much more did Grady know about her than she realized?

All day she'd been convinced he didn't know her well enough to marry her. That he'd been impulsive and hadn't thought out what married life would really be like. But now, she had to wonder…

Maybe she was the one who didn't know him.

"I CAN'T BELIEVE they found marshmallow roasting sticks." Melanie shifted beside him on the blanket he'd spread out in front of the fireplace for their makeshift picnic.

She still wore a white hotel spa robe, the fabric covering her from neck to toe, but she'd belted the thing so tight it accentuated her generous curves in a way that made him crazy. And when she leaned forward to find the hottest spot for her marshmallow… he didn't dare savor the view when the neckline gapped or she'd be back on the other side of the blanket in a heartbeat.

His wedding night was going to kill him.

"The tougher part was finding a property with a wood burning fireplace." He'd had to search fast, but he'd found just what he'd been looking for. And yeah, it helped that he had the money to pay for this place. He'd worked hard and made sacrifices for his career. Why shouldn't he enjoy the rewards? "I'm hoping I can convince you that camping in a luxury hotel can be all kinds of fun."

"You're making a heck of a case." She turned her marshmallow after one side charred dark brown, her cheeks pink from the warmth of the blaze. "I like the ant-free picnic."

Score. He needed to start wooing her. Winning her back. He had three days before the regular season started, and he couldn't afford to chase her around central Florida for too long. As much as he wanted to smooth aside the terry cloth robe to bare her knee and kiss his way up her thigh, he needed to focus. Show her he understood what she liked—outside the bedroom—and prove they had what it took to stay together forever.

With an effort, he redirected his thoughts away from her body wrapped in just a robe.

"I'm glad you're having fun." He could see the other side

of her marshmallow was about to catch flame and reached for her stick. "Can I get that for you?"

At her nod, he took the long metal fork with a wood handle on the end, the prong looking like something out of a fondue set. Carefully, he eased it away from the flames.

"Watch out for Polly," she reminded him.

The pup had fallen asleep with her furry chin on a dog biscuit—mid gnaw. Now, she snoozed on the far corner of the picnic blanket.

"I see her." Still, he was careful about where he laid aside the hot metal fork after he slid the gooey marshmallow onto a plate to cool. "Do you mind if I ask you a question about your family?"

"A question?" Melanie's eyes shot to his. She shifted from her spot on the leather ottoman to a seat beside him on the quilt.

Putting her in touchable range, even though she looked a little freaked out at the idea of talking about her family.

"I'm camping and testing out life as a pet owner, right? I'm trying to compromise. So it's your turn. Share some of your secrets that you think are going to keep us apart."

"I didn't mean to keep them a secret—"

"Yes you did." He watched the flames glow blue at the base of the blaze, figuring it was safer to keep an eye on the flames than her.

"Okay, maybe I did. But you know I work in my father's restaurant a lot of nights."

"I know it's on the other side of town from the ball field and that you discouraged me from stopping by."

"Dad's sort of a local legend. A minor league journeyman who hit a lot of homeruns but never went back to the majors after a shoulder injury prevented him from being as good as he once was."

He could sense a whole lot of subtext there, but wasn't quite sure how to pull it free.

"No wonder you know your baseball." He'd been impressed at her knowledge of the game more than once—from situational pitching to batter's box strategy. But she'd written it off as stuff she'd picked up on her temp jobs at the training facility.

"Baseball and broken dreams. They're the language of the household." The bitterness in her voice was something he'd never heard.

"Your dad took it hard?" He wanted to understand her better. Wished he'd worked harder to figure her out sooner.

"Not as hard as Mom did. Her disappointment in him drove her to drink. For a long time, I thought he was crazy to stay with her. But as I get older, I think it's how he punishes himself."

"That's so—"

"Dysfunctional? Messed up? Yeah. I know."

He shook his head. "I was going to say, that's sort of like my father. He was an angry man and he took it out in the boxing ring as a small-time fighter. He always wanted his sons to do better. Be more than the old man. So he drilled us relentlessly on our chosen sports. Baseball for me. Golf for Seth. Hit two hundred balls before dinner. Two hundred more before bed."

"Yet you always credit your father with your success as a player." She frowned, her eyes full of tender concern.

"I wouldn't be where I am without him. Although if I had it to do over, I'd be a golfer like Seth."

"He's on the PGA tour, isn't he?"

"Yes, but I don't envy his success as much as the fact that he always got to hit his two hundred balls off the tee. Whereas I got the old man pitching to me for most of those swings. Which meant I doubled up on the father-son time." He shook off the old ghosts. "But if you're thinking I'm some kind of sports fanatic, I can tell you nothing could be further from the truth. When my career is over, I move on—no regrets."

Her eyes darted away.

"However long the success lasts, you pay a high price for it." She picked up her marshmallow now that it had cooled, balancing it on her fingertips while she seemed to debate how to eat it.

"Damn straight. And I'd never want to be with a woman who didn't understand that." He savored the sight of her tongue testing the gooey warmth.

Her eyes closed for a moment as she sampled the treat.

And just like that, the temperature in the room spiked.

The dynamic between them shifted. He'd known her long enough to feel the sexual hum of awareness, and he felt his restraint slide away. He'd missed her so much the night before. Had dreamed of being with her today—as husband and wife.

He must have made a sound. Or moved toward her. Because suddenly her eyes locked with his. Awareness sparked. Flamed.

"Want some?" She held out half the marshmallow to him, sticky white liquid encased in a flaky dark shell.

"I think you know I do." His eyes never left hers as he braced himself for a retreat.

"I don't like denying myself any more than you do," she confessed unhappily.

"So why do it?" He shoved aside leftover dishes. Tossed a towel next to Polly to keep her feeling safe. "I don't see how not touching each other is going to suddenly help us think more clearly. If anything, the wanting is a distraction that's tough to see past."

He kept his hands to himself, not making his case in the most convincing manner, but he was trying to be fair. Let her decide.

For a long moment, they stared at each other over the marshmallow, flames crackling in the fireplace beside them. And then, slowly, she nodded.

Only then did he take Melanie's hand and bring her fingers to his mouth, white sugar coating two of them. He heard her breathing quicken. Felt her pulse race under his thumb where he held her wrist.

She watched him, her lips parted, as he cleaned her fingers with his tongue. Slowly. Thoroughly. All the while, she breathed harder. Faster. Until her tongue darted out to trace along her upper lip and nearly undid him.

"I could eat you up." He spoke into her ear, his mouth grazing the impossible softness of her neck, then skimmed her lips. "But only if you want me to."

At the words, he felt Melanie turn rigid. The progress he thought they had been making was quickly fading.

"I…I can't, Grady." Her words were soft, barely spoken above a whisper against his mouth before she eased back out of his arms.

Her unmistakable conviction slammed into him. One kiss hadn't gained him anything more than to send her running again. Faster. She gathered Polly in her arms, shot to her feet, and retreated into the smaller bedroom. Leaving him alone. On his wedding night.

Damn it. This was not how he wanted things to be between them. He had to convince her that this was right. That they were right. If he could only just get her to talk to him. To trust him.

He fought the urge to charge after her. Moving too fast was what had gotten them into this mess in the first place. He would let her sort through her feelings tonight. The day had been taxing on both of them. But tomorrow…tomorrow he would resume his campaign to win her over.

ONCE THE DOOR was closed and locked behind her, she slumped onto the hotel bed, the plush duvet poofing underneath her. With a wet nose, Polly nudged her hand. Absently, Melanie scratched the puppy's head, finding calming and comfort in the animal's soft fur.

Of all the ways she had pictured her wedding night, this scenario had never entered her mind. There was a door between her and her husband. A door she had put there. To protect herself. To protect him.

But that didn't make it any easier.

She hugged Polly closer as sobs clogged her throat and her nose burned with the tears building up inside her. She blinked hard to hold them back. But no luck. Tears mixed with the remainder of her eye shadow and mascara streaming down her cheeks. She slumped back into the pile of pillows, so much softer than a tent floor.

Good. She felt like she deserved it for causing the hurt to darken Grady's normally warm cinnamon eyes. He was so kind, so generous. But she was all wrong for him. She couldn't be the one to tie this man down to a future he didn't want. Melanie wouldn't do that.

She refused to continue to cause him pain. It was too cruel, too selfish to hang onto this marriage they'd jumped into so fast. Which is why he needed to leave now before she caused him any more damage.

But what about her pain? This wasn't how things were supposed to be. Weddings were happy occasions. And she had made such a grand mess out of it all.

Another sob caused her to shudder. Polly whimpered, then licked Melanie's arm. Through her blurry vision, she could make out the puppy's sympathetic eyes. The tears eased, the puppy's comfort bolstering her enough to regain some control.

"What am I doing, Polly?" As if in response, the puppy cocked her head, trying to make sense of her question. She let out a small bark before curling up in a tight ball on the bed, tail wagging now that Melanie had stopped crying.

"If only it were that simple, little one," Melanie breathed, lying next to the dog.

Part of her wanted Grady. His kiss. His heat. There was an undeniable chemistry between them. There had been since the moment they met. But that kind of chemistry didn't mean that they could build a life together.

It wasn't fair to either of them. She had to leave, had to show this too-good-for-her man that they were on two completely different—and incompatible—paths. But how was she supposed to get that point across to him so he wouldn't keep following her? She scratched Polly's head, searching for more of that calm and peace to sort through her thoughts.

The pup had fallen asleep curled against Melanie, her little chest rhythmically rising and falling. Polly needed a real collar, one that suited her. Melanie envisioned something cute, fun, something that fit a helluva lot better than her wedding dress had. Maybe she would go tomorrow morning to look for a collar and leash before Grady woke up since the last thing he would want to do on his honeymoon would be shop for doggy paraphernalia. The extra time alone could give her time to think. Time to figure out how to show Grady why their marriage was a mistake. But as she glanced at the sleeping puppy, the perfect plan began to take shape in her mind, thanks to Polly and that missing collar. She kissed the puppy between her ears. Polly stretched her paws out, still half asleep.

The best way to show him that their marriage would never work? Paint the domestic scene. His life as a rising baseball star wasn't a good fit for her ideas on the future. She wanted to plant roots somewhere, wanted kids, and a house that needed weekend projects. That vision would send him away. It would help him move on.

So she would preview that life. Tomorrow at the pet store.

# Chapter Five

"WELL, THIS IS just adorable," Melanie breathed in the center of the pet store. She held up a pink leopard print leash. Her lips pursed as she scrutinized the details along the length.

As Melanie inspected yet another leash, Grady glanced around the store, his foot twitching from boredom. How long did it take to choose a leash and collar, for Pete's sake? And how much stuff did one puppy need?

He studied the other shoppers to gauge. A family with a harnessed husky mix stood at the opposite end of the aisle. A little boy, four at most, gave the husky a giant hug while the parents picked up a few toys, balls, bones, and tossed them in the cart. There was a look exchanged between the couple, one that broadcasted their love, their commitment to being on the same team. It was that look he was after with Melanie.

One that seemed impossible to obtain as the day wore on and she vetoed his choices while she held up each option against the pup's fur to look for the perfect match.

"But this one doesn't say 'Polly' either, does it?" she

sighed setting the leash back down on the rack. He turned away from the family to study her.

This was the seventh leash Melanie had ogled. And the seventh one she had rejected. Grady took a steadying breath, doing his best to keep his frustration in check.

They had already been in the pet store for an hour. And the only item in the cart was a bag of kibble. Melanie's attention flitted between cutesy items for the puppy so fast, he could barely keep up.

Grady balanced in a squat, petting Polly, who rolled over to accommodate a good belly-rub. Her tongue lolled lazily out of her mouth with unmistakable bliss.

"Oh Grady. What about this?" Melanie said, a smile on her face as she held up a purple doggie-hoodie that read "puppy love" in white cursive letters.

"It's nice. But Polly is going to be growing like a weed. I don't know if—" He stopped talking as he examined her face.

Tears welled in her eyes. And she seemed to retreat into herself farther. Damn it.

With a sigh, Grady forged ahead. "You know what? That's perfect. Toss it in."

He pushed the cart towards her. She plopped the sweater inside, a smile deepening the dimples in her cheeks.

Turning back to the leashes, she picked up a purple leather one.

"Now we have a theme. She'll be a vision in purple," she

said as she tossed the leash and matching collar into the cart.

They made it five more steps before she stopped again.

"Look. At. These. Toys," she squealed, running her hands across the arrangement of squeaky stuffed animals.

There was such an exaggeration in her voice. It didn't add up. None of her behavior today aligned with the Melanie he knew and loved.

She seemed to be waiting for him to comment. A little *too* eagerly for this to be part of a normal conversation.

A thought tugged at him. Was she trying to push him away again? To become a pouty girl when he disagreed. While he had been blind to how freaked out she was about their marriage, he knew this wasn't the real Melanie.

If she was trying to scare him off with overplayed domesticity, the least he could do was give her a run for her money. It was worth an experiment at the very least. Time to knock her off balance for a change.

"There are a lot of toys," he said enthusiastically. "How many do you think she needs? Ten? Fifteen? We will need a variety of toys that squeak, and some toys that don't. And of course, a Frisbee! Every dog needs a Frisbee. That would be great for camping trips. And speaking of camping trips, look at those outdoor dog beds that can be anchored to the ground. Perfect for camping."

She gaped at him, brows raised in complete surprise. It was only for a moment, but it told him everything he needed to know. This was an exaggeration, an act. He was sure of that now. She chewed her lip for a moment, turning sideways to let an older couple walking a lab mix walk past before she turned back to him with an over-bright smile.

"Yes. Let's get ten toys. That is the perfect number," she said removing a variety of toys from the shelves.

"What about a dog bed for indoors as well?" he asked, gesturing in front of them to the back wall where a middle-aged women held a toy poodle in her arms as she examined the beds. The poodle stared at Polly and barked excitedly.

"Hush now." The blonde lady soothed the black poodle, "That nice golden isn't bothering you." She glanced over at them. "She gets excited easily."

"Please don't worry," Melanie said, "we want to socialize Polly. She won't be an only dog for long."

"Oh," the woman exclaimed, "How exciting. Is this your first dog together?"

Grady nodded. "Yes, ma'am."

The woman looked wistfully at them, shaking her head at the memory of things past. "I remember what it was like when Bobby and I got our first dog. That pup taught us so much, though I think it's supposed to be the other way around. No matter, y'all enjoy the pup and each other."

She hugged her poodle closer with one hand and pushed her shopping buggy with the other towards the front of the store. Had Melanie heard the woman's words? Taken them to heart? Grady turned to his wife, but she was already debating between two dog beds.

"Which one?" She held up a large bed that was lined with fleece and one that was lined with microfiber.

"You pick," he said, the game suddenly losing some of its fun as he thought about the sadness in the lonely woman's eyes.

"This one," Melanie said, holding up the microfiber bed, "is much softer. Oh, the decisions we have to make for you, Polly."

At the mention of her name, the dog surged forward, against her newly fitted collar.

Grady couldn't take his eyes off Melanie. She was beautiful. Nurturing. Everything he wanted. Everything he needed. Even when she was trying to push him away.

"Maybe we should let Polly choose. We'll take whatever she sniffs first. But let's do it quickly. I have a surprise." He yanked at his phone and went to work.

A QUICK INTERNET search had revealed the location of the local dog park where Grady insisted on taking Polly. Melanie still tried to wrap her brain around how quickly he'd gotten on board with the doggy parenting outing. Now, he insisted he wanted to make sure the pup was properly exercised. This didn't fit with the party animal image she'd had of him as a pro athlete.

What game was he playing? Or was this the real man and

she hadn't noticed before?

They were the only ones at the wooded park. It was a perfect retreat with shady trees and benches. Away from reality. From the pressure of anything outside of caring for this adorable puppy.

She watched Grady intently as he made sure Polly had water. His broad back was to her, and his shoulders were relaxed. The fresh air was doing them all some good.

"You know, for never owning a dog, you're practically a natural," she called to him. Grady had been working with Polly for the better part of a half hour on the sit command.

"Thanks, I was even careful to find a less visited park so she wouldn't be exposed to germs from other dogs since she's so young," he said, a smile widening across his face as he turned to face her. Polly's tail wagged in anticipation of the training treats. She twitched her feet in anticipation but stayed sitting. "Good girl."

He rewarded her with the treat. The pup chewed it happily.

"What a good puppy," Melanie cooed as the dog pranced up to her.

Those warm cinnamon eyes met hers, twinkling with a compassion and love that she had never quite noticed before. Without question, he was thoroughly enjoying this low-key day. She'd misjudged him on this point.

And what other things might she have mistaken?

Melanie turned her focus back to Polly. "Here you go,

girlie," she said, tossing one of the newly purchased toys – a braided rope ball – out into the still-vacant dog park.

"And you don't have a bad throwing arm," he observed, still smiling at her. Polly took off at a near-gallop after the toy, kicking up dirt and grass as she went to the edge of the park.

"I can thank my dad for that. He thought it was an important skill for me to have. Probably because it was a way for him to still enjoy the game."

He nodded thoughtfully at her.

The dog returned with her roped ball, tail wagging all the way back to them, clearly proud of herself. Polly dropped the toy in front of Grady, ready to go again. He sent the ball flying and she took off again. They did this routine five more times and he never once seemed annoyed.

He was patient, reassuring. Everything that was important in a pet owner.

*Or a future father,* a small voice inside of her called. How she wanted that to be true. A lump formed in her throat.

She couldn't let herself think like that though. It was too soon for her to go that far in her thoughts.

She hitched her purse on her shoulder. "I'm ready for some dinner. Maybe we can get room service again?"

He raised his brow, scooping up the ball and puppy. "Yeah, of course. A night in will be just what we need. Besides, I think Polly is exhausted. She'd probably appreciate some downtime as well."

Tucking Polly against his chest, he opened the park gates on their way back to the car, the sun setting and casting a mellow glow over the end of a surprisingly great day.

Melanie gave a quick nod as she opened the passenger side door. "Perfect. I think I want that spinach and cheese dip again."

"That can most certainly be arranged." A crooked grin notched in the corner of his mouth as he secured Polly in the back seat with a newly purchased doggie harness seat belt.

Sliding back into the driver's seat, he turned on the ignition. "Mind if I put some music on?"

She shook her head, curious what he would pick. Curious about so much more when it came to her new husband. Grady fiddled with the radio, settling on an old country love ballad. He hummed along. Didn't press her to talk. The silence felt…comfortable. Easy.

His hand slid to the top of her thigh. The warmth from his palm felt delicious on her bare skin. It was such a simple gesture, so sweet. Her thoughts turned back to the course of the day, to the surprisingly good time they'd had.

They were silent on the way back to the hotel. Melanie barely registered the walk back to the room. She was preoccupied with how wonderful their day had been. And that was a problem.

It was time to regain control. To regroup. To guard her heart against this practically perfect man.

GRADY TIPPED THE room service delivery attendant, and turned back to Melanie, who was curled up on the couch, remote in hand. God, she was gorgeous in that thick robe, her hair loose and damp around her shoulders.

"I've picked out a movie for us to watch over dinner." She clicked play on the remote and ordered the movie off of pay-per-view.

"Excellent. That's my favorite way to unwind." He brought the tray over to the coffee table in front of her. There were two orders of spinach and cheese dip. The accompanying chips were piled high, nearly spilling over the side of the bowl.

He sat next to her, pressing his leg against hers.

Her pulse leapt. "I imagine you prefer high action, shoot-em-ups."

"Not so much," he said truthfully. "I like period pieces, old films, and documentaries."

"Really? You're a movie buff? Where does that fit in with your major-league, fast track lifestyle?" She chased around a chunk of cheese with a chip, scooping the heap ungracefully into her mouth.

"What does my career have to do with a love of old movies?" Try as he might, he couldn't work out the accusatory statement and stare.

Melanie's shoulders shrugged. "Don't you spend your

evenings going to parties with the team?"

"Not if I can help it. That's a fast way to burn out or tick off the manager." He licked his fingers.

"Uhm, okay. I can see that." She channel surfed, frowning.

"Wait! Stop!" His head whipped toward the screen at the familiar sound. "Is this *High Society*?"

"Yeah. Lame, I know. It's one of my favorites. So romantic. And I do love the singing." Her tone fell low, "You probably hate this kind of thing, don't you?"

There she went again. Assuming so many things about him. Maybe, just maybe, if he could open up a little bit more to her, she would realize they were more alike. That there was common ground between them. That he meant his vows.

"I meant it when I said I love classic movies, but this is probably in my top ten." He laughed out. "I know all of those songs by heart."

"Really?" Eyebrow arched in disbelief.

Grady's arm snaked behind her head, and rested on her shoulders, allowing himself to toy with a lock of her damp hair. "Truly. When you are on the road for weeks on end, you have the opportunity to watch a lot of television and movies. Which I wholeheartedly take advantage of. I skip out on parties in favor of some old-fashioned relax time."

"You are a man of pleasant surprises. I'll give you that much," she teased. A genuine smile spread across her face.

Nestling against his chest, she sighed deeply.

"I do try. What other movies do you love?" His hand gently pushed hair from her face, and he began to massage her scalp.

"Hmmm." She practically purred. "That's nice."

He damned well hoped so, because just the feel of her was turning him inside out. The movie rolled along, the songs filling in the small spaces of their conversation. They were more alike than even he had realized.

This felt so right. He ached to be closer to her. To keep them in this moment forever. Kissing her on the forehead, he released a deep sigh.

Pushing off his chest, she stared at him, eyes intense. Full of longing.

"Oh, Grady," she whispered, "I give up."

She kissed him. Deeply.

And then again. More urgently this time.

"Are you sure, Mel?" he said between kisses. "I don't want you regretting this. God, we don't need any more regrets."

He didn't want to rush this. Wouldn't let her think he'd ignored her concerns. But the chemistry between them was a vivid, hot, sexual need that wouldn't go away if they ignored it.

"I'm unsure about many things. But about this?" She nodded, the movement swift. Jerky. "I am one hundred percent certain I want you. Now."

She flattened herself against him, her full breasts robbing him of his last shred of sense.

"You've always felt right to me." He whispered it to himself as much as her. "Exactly right."

MELANIE COULDN'T REMEMBER why she wanted to deny herself this.

Grady was a potent, sexual male even when he stood in a batter's box or ran down a fly ball in the field. But when he sat this close to her, his brown eyes searing her with silent, simmering heat, he was a temptation no woman would ever resist. That powerful body of his. That demanding mouth. She wanted all of it for however long this fever between them lasted.

Tomorrow would come soon no matter what happened in this hotel room.

She kissed him. The barriers between them melted like they'd never been there, her defenses crumbling as fast as his. Not that she'd ever had any with this man. From the first night they met, passion seethed just beneath the surface all the time. The slightest touch could turn her inside out. Or the taste of a marshmallow could transform into an erotic experience because he was watching. Before Grady, she'd barely been orgasmic. With Grady? She could reach that peak again and again in a single night.

He bent her back over his arm, kissing her like he was starved for her. She clung to him like he was the only thing keeping her anchored to the world. Impatient hands tore away the cloth belt holding her robe closed and in an instant, she was naked against him.

The shock of his body—ripped, hard, male perfection—made her breasts bead against his chest. Her thighs heated with a liquid ache.

She broke their kiss.

"You need to be naked." With unsteady fingers, she gripped the drawstring of his shorts and tugged. "Now."

"I can make that happen." He reached for the hem of his shirt and drew the tee up and off.

She forgot what she was doing for a moment to enjoy the show. Leaning closer, she kissed the tattoo of a smoking hot baseball bat on his biceps. He tasted like salt, soap and man. Perfect.

Taking a random path down his chest, she licked along the outline of more colorful ink—an impossible staircase that led in circles, geometric fractals. She went lower as he stepped out of his shorts and kicked aside his boxers. Lips moving along the proud thrust of manhood, she licked the ridge until he gripped her shoulders.

"I've missed you too much for that." The hoarse rasp of his voice pleased her.

She smiled up at him. "We were only apart two nights."

"And it was too long." He scraped back her hair with one

hand and tilted her chin up to look at him. "Come here."

Teasing him, she kept an eye on him as she circled the tip of him with her tongue....

She yelped as he lifted her in his arms, spinning her around until she realized he was carrying her to his bedroom.

Cool sheets enveloped her while he paused to find a condom. Sheathe himself. Then his hard body covered hers.

He sank into her. Deep.

Her breath caught. Her heart stuttered to a stop for a second before it began again at a frantic pace. She bit his shoulder for a moment before she realized what she was doing. Letting go, she tucked her forehead to his chest and wrapped her legs around his waist to hold him close.

He stroked her hair with one hand even as he stroked her insides with powerful thrusts. Opening her eyes, she peered up at him, visible in the moonlight streaming through a skylight over the bed. He was so beautiful it hurt to look at him. Not just because he was a sexy baseball star. But because she loved him.

Always.

Meeting his gaze for a long moment, he bent over her to take her mouth and kiss the ever-loving hell out of her. She let him, meeting his tongue stroke for stroke, rolling over him until she sat on top. Her hair fell forward, a dark curtain that closed out anything but their kiss.

There was a hushed, awed quality to lovemaking that had never been there before. She felt it in the way he moved against her. In the way he looked at her. It was because it was their first time together as a married couple. And he treated her with a level of reverence that she couldn't afford to think about right now.

Shaky, she straightened.

She fought for words that would dispel some of the seriousness that would make sex light and playful again. But Grady sat up with her so that she sat in his lap, straddling him intimately.

"I want to keep you in the moonlight." He edged her back under the skylight, keeping them sealed together as he spun her beneath him again. "You're so beautiful."

Dizzy from the spinning and the heady words, she could only clutch at his shoulders as he went to work on her breasts, lavishing them with kisses she could feel everywhere in her oversensitive skin. He plucked at her sex with his thumb and forefinger, catapulting her into a thousand sparks of delicious fulfillment. Then he did it all over again until she held him too tightly to let him do that again.

"Please," she whispered in his ear. Needing him to come with her the next time. Wanting to feel him burn the way she was burning.

Then he moved inside her and she couldn't think anymore. She could only hold on tight as he took them higher. Higher.

When she flew apart this time, he went with her, their shouts muffled against each other's shoulders, the heat sealing them together in a molten flame. Pleasure filled her to her fingertips, a languid, satiated joy that pulled her mouth into a smile. Lying beside him in the dark she tipped her forehead against his chest, snuggling close.

She wasn't sure how long they'd lain intertwined in his bed when his cell phone rang, the shrill chime jarring her out of half-formed dreams of lying beside him forever.

Beside her, Grady rolled off the bed with a grunted apology that she was too languid to answer. She tugged the sheet around her and curled into the warmth of where their bodies had been together. The scent of his aftershave lingered on the pillow.

When he returned to the bedroom a moment later, his scowl chilled the last of the warmth from their lovemaking.

Sitting up, she clutched the sheet around her. "Grady? What's wrong?"

He dropped to sit on the side of the bed, cell phone cradled in his hands, tendons in his neck strained. "Someone at the courthouse and a picture of our marriage certificate landed on social media."

"Oh no." She tucked the sheet tighter around her, trying to think through what that and their inevitable breakup meant for him. For his career. "I hadn't thought about that."

"Right. You didn't think the wedding would happen." His face was scrubbed clean of expression as he scooped up his shirt from the floor and pulled it on over his head. "But I'll need to deal with the fallout."

"What do you mean?" She felt his retreat, and it didn't have anything to do with him heading for the door.

"Considering all the questions the team is fielding about us since the story broke, the Stars rescinded their permission for me to drive to Atlanta." He retrieved his overnight bag and starting pitching in his belongings. "I need to be on the team plane so I can handle this with the press secretary in Atlanta tomorrow. We fly out at dawn."

# Chapter Six

GRADY HAD THE hotel room packed in record time, even making room for Polly in the back seat in a pet carrier they'd gotten from the vet. He'd offered to call a cab so Melanie didn't have to drive back to Orlando with him, but she'd insisted on going with him.

Not for a minute did he think that meant she'd decided to be his wife for real, however. He hadn't forgotten the talk of annulments the night before and he wasn't foolish enough to think that great sex would change her mind. Hell, they'd had great sex for a few weeks and she hadn't taken his proposal seriously in the first place. Why would he think she'd want to attend a press conference with him as his bride just because they'd shared another night together?

"I'm sorry about this." She sat in the passenger seat of the Honda, wearing jeans and a yellow tee that said "You are my Florida sunshine."

Something about that made his mood all the blacker since it felt like false advertising. She wasn't the easygoing, fun-loving woman he'd fallen for. By her own admission, she was more complicated than that. She'd hidden things from him. And she didn't want to be a "part time" wife. So basically, screw him and his proposal.

Screw their whole short-lived marriage.

"You didn't leak the photo." He'd switched off his phone half an hour ago when he realized how big of a deal this marriage had become in social media.

"But if we'd had a regular marriage, all of this would be easier because we'd face this together." She cleared her throat. "Like a couple."

"Yeah. We would." He drummed a beat on the steering wheel, not sure how much more he could risk his heart with this woman. She'd turned his life upside down in the last twenty-four hours.

Still, he wondered if he could have convinced her to stay with him if they'd had more time.

"I can take Polly though," she offered. "I've got room for her at my old apartment. They allow pets."

"How convenient. You can go right back to your old life now that I'm leaving." He shook his head. "But no thanks. I'm taking Polly with me. I paid the vet bill. She's in my name. She's my dog. End of discussion."

He felt her frown even though he stared straight ahead at the Florida Turnpike. He'd send someone to pick up his truck tomorrow. He'd be lucky to make it to the private airstrip for the plane at six a.m. For now, he just followed the red glow of taillights on the highway ahead and tried not to think about this season stretching out in front of him—one hundred and eighty some games that wouldn't be any fun without her.

"You can't care for a dog on the road."

"Like hell I can't." He actually had no idea how he was going to take the puppy with him, but he wasn't going to start this season alone. He might not have Melanie, but he would have his dog. "I'll get a pet sitter when I need to."

"A full time pet sitter. To travel with you."

"If that's what it takes. Yes."

"Are you sure that's fair to Polly?"

This time, he did turn to look at Melanie, illuminated by the dashboard lights. She toyed with the ribbon on the bridal bouquet he'd bought for her, curling the pink satin around one finger.

"You know how I knew you liked peonies?" he asked, ignoring the questions about the puppy since he hadn't thought that through yet.

"*I* didn't even know I liked peonies." She lowered her nose to the delicate petals and sniffed. "But they smell amazing."

"They're planted at the ballpark. That first night we danced in the rain in the dark, we were close to them. You said something smelled good and I asked the landscaper about them the next day. Peonies, he told me."

"Grady." Her voice broke. "I know I haven't been fair."

He gripped the steering wheel in white-knuckled fists, staring straight ahead. "What if I stayed here with you? Told the Stars I'd buy back my contract and—"

"No one does that." She shook her head in disbelief, her silky hair sliding over her shoulder just as it had slid over his body last night. "You don't turn your back on talent like yours."

"Hypothetically speaking, then." He had to know the answer to a question that had bothered him deep in his gut since he'd seen her sprint away. "If I was a regular guy you met at the field. Just another baseball fan. Would it be different right now? Would I know your parents or have a real wife?"

She blinked fast, looking away and outside the window so long he wasn't sure she would answer. Her chest moved with a heavy sigh. "I'm not sure this will make sense to you, but nobody ever put me first before. I didn't believe it was real because I didn't know what that felt like. So, no. I don't think it would have been any different. I still wouldn't have trusted what we had was real."

He'd asked for honesty and he'd gotten it, so he couldn't complain when it hurt like hell. She wouldn't have given him her heart no matter what he did. Maybe that should have made him feel better, but it burned a hole straight through him and left him raw. Empty.

Fresh out of words and realizing exactly how small his chances were of ever winning her over, Grady focused on getting to the airfield as fast as the law allowed. He'd shown her that he cared. That he loved her and wanted her in his life. She just didn't love him enough to want to be his wife.

When he pulled into the private airstrip where the team plane waited, he shoved the car into park but he didn't get out fast enough. Melanie took his hand and pressed something cold in his palm.

Her wedding ring.

"I'm sorry, Grady." At least her voice choked on the words. "Truly, I am."

Grinding his teeth, he took it and dropped it in the Honda's cupholder.

"I got it for you, Mel. Just like I got the house in Atlanta that I don't want anymore either. I'll sell our house, but you figure out what to do with the ring." The simple act of speaking hurt. Physically. Hurt. He reached in the backseat and pulled out Polly's carrier. "I'm taking our most important asset."

He eyed the Golden Retriever pup as she struggled to stay upright in the moving crate. He knew exactly how that balancing act felt and the dog managed a whole hell of a lot better than him.

Around them, he could see other players' cars pulling into the dark parking lot. He'd purposely put the Honda in a space farther from the team aircraft just in case there were any media gathered, but it looked quiet enough.

"Grady—" Melanie had slipped out of the passenger seat and stood across the hood from him.

But the time for talking was over. He had his answers

now.

"Let's at least end this honestly." He didn't know how he'd stand on a press podium and talk about her to the media in a few hours' time when it hurt this much just looking at her. "I'll look into an annulment when I get to Atlanta. Goodbye, Melanie."

He thought he saw a glint of tears on her cheeks, but it was probably a trick of the lights. Turning on his heel, he shouldered his overnight bag and took his dog to start the regular season without his wife.

MELANIE WATCHED HIM leave and wondered if he'd felt like this when she ran out of the courthouse two days ago.

*This was how it felt to watch the person you love most in the world walk away from you.*

The hurt was worse than anything she'd ever felt, and she'd taken a lacrosse ball to the eye socket in gym class once. Then there'd been the time her mother had accidentally punched her in the jaw a few years ago when she'd been going for Melanie's father. But seeing Grady stride off toward the plane—knowing how much she'd hurt him even though she loved him—hit a level of pain that all but doubled her over.

She didn't deserve him. Hadn't believed he loved her. Yet, somehow, he wanted her as much—maybe even more—

than he wanted a career in the majors. After a lifetime of reverberations in her family from her father's inability to make it on a major league roster, that simply hadn't computed in her brain. But was it so hard to believe that just maybe her family experience was wildly dysfunctional? That she'd been given a false view of love, marriage and sensible priorities?

What was she doing playing referee for her parents at her age, anyhow? She deserved her own life. A chance to make her own choices.

The knowledge that she was making the biggest mistake of her life cinched her chest like a vise. Her gaze dropped to the diamond ring in the cupholder and she leaned into the Honda to retrieve the double bands. She squeezed it so tight the setting imprinted on her skin. Fear of hurting Grady even more weighed her down like lead. An even bigger fear of losing him forever forced one foot in front of the other anyhow. She didn't know what she'd say when she caught up to him. But panic fluttered inside her with the urge to try something. Anything.

The time for small ball and a safe at-bat was long gone. She was down to her last out.

"Grady!" she called, feet kicking up gravel in the parking lot as she outran the glow of her headlights. "Wait!"

"Sorry, ma'am." A big, burly man stepped into her path from out of nowhere to shine a flashlight on her face. "No unauthorized parties past this point."

"I'm not unauthorized." She squinted past the flashlight beam as the security guard's name badge came into view. "Stephen?"

She recognized him from odd jobs around the spring training facility. They'd both been assigned to lay pavers in a walking path behind right field two years ago.

"Hey, Melanie. I didn't know that was you." He clicked off the flashlight. "What are you doing here?"

"I'm – um. In charge of pets on the plane," she fibbed. "A couple of players are bringing animals with them and I'm taking care of them during the flight."

She sidled past him while he made a low whistle.

"Sweet gig!" He gave her a thumbs-up sign. "But I thought you married the second baseman yesterday? Was that, like, an Internet hoax?"

She could not let her marriage come down to that—a brief social media rumor stomped out with a press release in the cold light of dawn. There had been peonies.

And love.

"Actually, I really hope not." She pointed to the plane. "Do you mind if I—"

"Sure, sure." He waved her past. "Don't forget the little guys when you're a big deal player's wife, okay?"

She smiled at him even though his words made her stomach tighten painfully. She brushed past one of the other Stars, a lanky pitcher who towered over her as she neared the steps to the plane.

Taking the steps two at a time, she shot past the catcher, a Cuban built like a bulldog who stood joking with one of the other air hostesses in the aisle of the posh private jet.

"Grady?" she called, turning the heads of the handful of players already in their seats.

And then, she saw him. Middle of the plane. Bulky, noise-cancelling headphones already in place. He stared out the window next to him even though it was pitch black on that side of the aircraft.

"Excuse me, miss." A woman in a sharp navy suit approached her from the back of the plane. "I'm going to have to ask you to leave—."

One of the other players – Boone Sullivan – tapped Grady on the shoulder and pointed. Grady turned to face her, his eyes going wide with hope, then wariness.

Slowly, he removed the headset. "Melanie? Did you forget something?"

He didn't make a move to stand. Or to save her from the all-business-looking blonde in the tailored suit who still barreled toward her, a team VIP badge around her neck.

"Sorry." Melanie attempted to smile at the VIP but the woman's expression didn't change. Instead, Melanie tried her luck with Grady. "Actually, Grady. I did forget something." She struggled for what to say. For how to express herself to him in front of one pissed-off looking team representative and ten Stars teammates he'd have to play with all season.

"And?" He looked at her with a touch of weariness, no

doubt as exhausted from the last forty-eight hours as she felt.

But then, he didn't know that her whole life rested on this moment and that gave her the courage to finally blurt what was in her heart.

"I forgot to tell you that I'd rather be your part time wife than anyone else's full time bride. Because the kind of love I feel for you is enough to fill however long we have to spend apart."

A few snickers in the aisle behind her. Navy Suit Woman sighed impatiently like she'd heard a million such declarations from infatuated females.

The only person's reaction who mattered, however, remained expressionless.

He put aside the headset but stayed seated, his eyes still full of hurt that stabbed her clean through. "Since you don't seem inclined to be married in the first place, Mel, I'm not sure that's such a resounding endorsement."

He hadn't booted her off the plane though. And he was listening.

She blocked out all the eagerly listening ears around her and tried not to think about all the leaks to the press, possibly even a team reporter taking notes. "I spent a lifetime becoming the screwed up woman you see standing before you now. I wasn't ready to undo it all in the course of a day. And literally, that's as long as I've allowed myself to really think that a future between us might be true. That you and I could really… beat the odds. Become a winning team." She swallowed hard and laid it all on the line. "I love you, Grady."

One of the new rookies--some immature kid – snorted.

Grady scowled and shot out of his seat, jostling the younger guy hard with his shoulder. "Sorry about that, kid. My footing was knocked off balance by your rudeness to my wife."

*His wife.*

She'd never heard more beautiful words.

Grady plowed forward, bracing one hand at a time on the seats as he walked the aisle. Toward her. Like a reverse of a wedding march. "Let's find somewhere more private."

A whistle sailed up into the cabin.

The VIP lady stopped them both. "Mr. and Mrs. Hollis, I'm afraid you'll both to have to sit down and buckle in for takeoff. I assume you're both staying on the plane? Attending the press conference in Atlanta together?"

Melanie thought briefly of her car parked outside, and then forgot all about her past. She was looking at her future and she didn't intend to let him get away for a second time.

Grady looked down at her. "Well, Mel? Are we?"

She nodded enthusiastically. "We most definitely are."

"Good," Ms. VIP said in a clipped tone, belied by a twinkle in her eyes. Or maybe she was just glad that her press event just got a whole lot easier. "I happen to have two seats alone on a row. If you'll come this way." She paused to point at the pet carrier next to Grady's former seat. "And, maybe, bring the dog with you?"

And before she could say uber-efficient, Melanie found herself seated beside Grady in the very back, away from prying eyes for the most part. Major rules had been broken for her to be on this plane. Wives didn't ride on the team plane—it was a once-in-a-lifetime occurrence. But the Stars made an exception this once. For them. Maybe this team really did care about each other when it mattered most.

Melanie settled the sleeping puppy's carrier on the floor between their feet and straightened.

"I meant what I said to you, Grady." She was sure of this. Of them.

She'd just needed a little time to wrap her head around it.

"I know you do." He stroked back her hair with a gentle reverent hand. "And I meant every word I said to you in the courthouse. I want to be your husband, to honor and cherish you. To love you for the rest of my life."

She saw the truth in his eyes. Allowed herself to see. And was so grateful for this second chance. She placed her hands on his dear, handsome face and kissed him once, twice, saying between each kiss, "We'll make this work. I know we can."

He took her hand in his, his thumb working over where she'd put her rings back on. "We will. And we're going to do this right, planning for our future even after my traveling days are over. I mean it when I say, you let me know if the life's too much for you."

"It won't be." She could handle this. She'd plowed through so many unhappy days in her life, she could definitely start thinking about fun times ahead. Smiling and laughing more. Living the rest of her life as happily as the last ten weeks.

"I know it will take time. Some adjustments. But we've got options. We have the house in Atlanta, but we'll keep a home here too, in Orlando."

"I'd like that." Her heart was so full she thought it might burst. She tipped her forehead to his. Kissed his cheek. "You know, I've been considering what you said about my traveling with you. I like the sound of that." The adventure. The sense that marriage didn't have to be like her parents'. "I'm quite adaptable, thanks to all those temp jobs. Who knows? Maybe now that I'm finally getting a degree soon, this will be the perfect time for me to plan for my future career too."

His smile stretched, brushing her lips. "I like the sound of that. I like the sound of you. In my life. In my heart."

The engines roared and the plane began to taxi as she said, "You have quite a way with words for a ballplayer."

"I might have a few years of experience charming the hometown press." He stroked her hair. Straightened her wedding ring on her finger and then kissed the place where it rested. "But I save all my best material for the woman I love."

"We're going to have the best marriage." She knew it

deep in her soul. She didn't know what she'd done right to deserve this man, but she wasn't letting him go. And she was going to love him like nobody's business. "And I'm going to be your full time pet sitter too."

"Is that right?" He kissed her eyes that had started to tear up from sheer happiness. "Maybe we'd better say our vows again. Have a long version of the wedding ceremony so we can tell each other all the ways we're going to be good to each other."

"We could." She loved that he offered. That he would do that for her. "But I don't need any more formal vows. I believe you when you say you're going to love me forever. I promise you, I'm going to love you right back."

"Well, in that case," he answered, sliding his arm around her shoulder and tucking her to his side, "we'll just concentrate on living the dream." He took out his phone to show her the photo of their Marriage Certificate that had caused a stir on social media. "Care to make it official for the fans, too?"

She fell in love with the challenge in his eyes, the devilry and daring that had swept her off her feet ten weeks ago.

"What do you have in mind?"

"A quick honeymoon selfie?" he asked, kissing her cheek and snapping a picture.

"Absolutely." Her heart warmed to see the image on his phone. They both glowed. "What shall we say?" She pointed to the comment box next to the picture he planned to post.

He typed a few words and showed it to her. "How about this?"

*My new MVP – meet the Mrs.*

Laughing, she tapped the Send button for him. Then, setting his phone aside, she went about kissing him and keeping her spot on the roster… forever.

# Epilogue

MELANIE SWIPED ON shimmery pink lip gloss in the bathroom of the restaurant. She was out for a low key evening on the town with her husband and two of their friends. Grady and Melanie had been married for a month. And they were closer than ever.

"Are you getting excited for the big day?" Melanie asked Annamae Jessup, Boone Sullivan's reality star fiancée.

Leaning against the sink, Annamae glanced at her ring before answering, a forced smile nudging at her lips. "Of course! It's going to be quite an event. I'm so glad you and Grady can attend."

Melanie nodded as she held the thick wooden door open for them both, hoping that Annamae and Boone could be even half as happy as she and Grady were. "We are too."

And she meant it. Despite the presence of Annamae's reality show crew, she and Boone were nice people. Normal people. No drama, no crazy partying nights. Melanie had been surprised to find there were couples with similar values and lifestyles to what she wanted. But then Grady had told her as much. She just hadn't been ready to listen.

She and Annamae returned to the boys at the table, sounds of old Italian singers mingling with the din of the restaurant's low conversations.

Grady's eyes lit up at the sight of her.

"Aren't they the two most beautiful ladies in Atlanta?" Grady whistled softly before planting a kiss on Melanie's lips.

His kiss still sent shivers down her spine and made her knees go weak, giving her the perfect excuse to sink into her chair.

Boone helped Annamae into her seat. "And we are the lucky guys that locked them down."

Melanie linked hands with her husband, so glad she'd taken the leap of faith to marry this man. It had been so simple to adjust into her life with Grady. Everything fit. She was moving forward with her degree, finding her passion in life. And Grady was there to support her, despite his hectic career.

Nothing about Melanie's life had ever been conventional. And neither had been their courtship...and yet, she was able to live the life she had been so afraid to hope for.

Their eyes met as Boone and Annamae discussed the details of their upcoming wedding. Melanie's thoughts wandered away from the present conversation to the man that was before her eyes. Her husband.

Her forever was with *him*. With this wonderful man who hadn't given up on her no matter how hard she'd tried to lose him. And she was excited for what the next month, the next year, the next few decades would bring for them both.

Their marriage? This was the big-leagues. They were the all-stars, along with Polly and the children they would have over the years, a team for the rest of her days.

THE END

If you enjoyed **How to Lose a Groom in 10 Days**, you'll love the next Runaway Bride stories!

**How to Lose a Groom in 10 Days**

Book 1: **The Wedding Audition**

Book 2: **There Goes the Bride**

Book 3: **Bride on the Run**

*Available now at your favorite online retailer!*

## ABOUT THE AUTHORS

*USA Today* bestseller and RITA Award winner, Catherine Mann writes contemporary romance for Berkley, Harlequin, Sourcebooks and Tule. With over sixty books in released in more than twenty countries, she has also celebrated six RITA finals, an RT Reviewer's Award finalist, three Maggie Award of Excellence finals and a Bookseller's Best win. A former theater school director and university instructor, she holds a Master's degree in Theater from UNC-Greensboro and a Bachelor's degree in Fine Arts: Theater (with minors in both English and Education) from the College of Charleston. Catherine and her flyboy husband live on the Florida coast where they brought up their 4 children – and still have 5 four-legged, furry "children" (aka pets). Visit Catherine's website at www.CatherineMann.com.

Joanne Rock writes romance of all shapes and sizes from sexy contemporary to medieval historical and an occasional Young Adult story. She's penned over seventy books, appearing most often in the Harlequin Blaze series. Joanne taught English at the college level before becoming a full-time writer, and she returns to the classroom as often as possible to share her love of stories. A quiet and unassuming Virgo, Joanne married a fiery and boisterous Aries man in true opposites-attract fashion. Visit her website at www.JoanneRock.com.

Thank you for reading

## HOW TO LOSE A GROOM IN 10 DAYS

If you enjoyed this book, you can find more from all our great authors at TulePublishing.com, or from your favorite online retailer.

CPSIA information can be obtained
at www.ICGtesting.com
Printed in the USA
LVHW03s1626241018
594668LV00003B/520/P